A LOUD WINTER'S NAP

by Katy Hudson

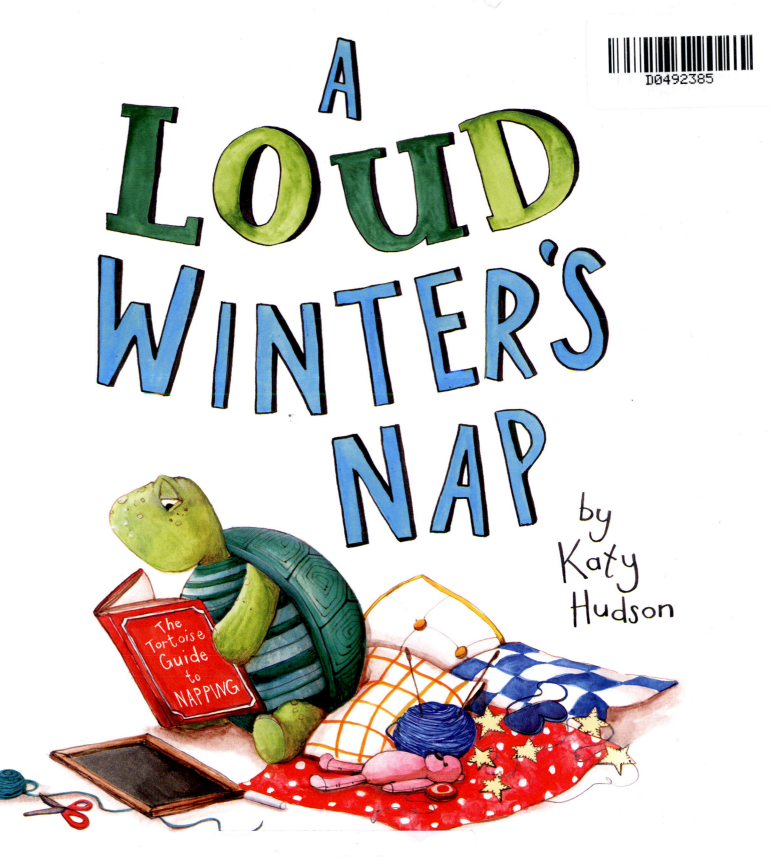

The Tortoise Guide to NAPPING

Tortoise
and the
Hare

BEDTIME
STORY
CLASSICS

For my Husband
and everything
you do. K.H. x

HIBERNATION
SOCIETY

Tortoi[se]

(hibernation)
/ˌhʌɪbəˈneɪʃ(ə)n/
noun
• The period of an
animal spending the
winter in a sleeping
state.

Fig1: Tortoise hibernating.

Winter

Fig 2: asleep

Fig 3: still asleep

Fig 4: still asleep

* Yet to be tested...

Tortoise sleeping
Activity:

All winter, the
Tortoise is in a
state of sleep/nap
until the weather
gets warmer in the
spring. They then
wake from their
big sleep and go to
sleep as normal.
They never see *
or like winter. *

In case
you get
peckish!
Love Rabbit
x

First published in 2017 by Curious Fox,
an imprint of Capstone Global Library Limited,
264 Banbury Road, Oxford, OX2 7DY – Registered
company number: 6695582

www.curious-fox.com

ISBN 978-1-78202-745-4

21 20 19 18 17
10 9 8 7 6 5 4 3 2 1

A CIP catalogue for this book is available from the
British Library.

Printed and bound in China.

Tortoise had just snuggled in for
his long winter nap when ...

"Hello there, Tortoise!" chirped Robin. "Would you like to join our singing class?"

"No," grumbled Tortoise. "I was trying to sleep. Tortoises don't like winter."

DO NOT DISTURB (until Spring)

TORTOISE

ROBI
WINT
SING
CLA

"Why not?" chirped Robin.

EVERY MORNING

Robin's
Winter
singing
class

Robin

"They just don't," said Tortoise. And he packed up
and left in search of a quieter home.

Tortoise snuggled down in his new bed. He was just about to close his eyes when ...

DO NOT DISTURB (until Spring)

Tap... Tap... Tap... TAP... Tap... Tap... TAP! TAP!

"Hiya, Tortoise! Would you like to make some ice sculptures with me?" asked Rabbit.

"No," groaned Tortoise. "I was trying to sleep. Tortoises don't like winter."

"Why not?" asked Rabbit.

"They just don't," said Tortoise. And he packed up again.

Tortoise trudged through the
snow and found a new napping
spot. Again, Tortoise snuggled
down in his new bed.

He was just about to close
his eyes when ...

"Hey, Tortoise! Would you like to play in our snowball fight?" asked Squirrel.

"No," Tortoise said angrily. "I'm trying to sleep. Tortoises don't like winter."

"Why not?" asked Squirrel.

"They just don't," groaned Tortoise.

"Why would anyone want to stay awake for winter?" grumbled Tortoise.

He was tired and cold and needed to find a quieter place to sleep. Tortoise decided to move to higher ground.

Grown by Rabbit

carrots

Beaver's tools

Again, Tortoise snuggled down in his new bed. He was just about to close his eyes when ...

Duh...

duuhhhhh!

Duh!

Duh!

Duhhh!

Duhhh!!!

Bounce!

Bounce!

Bounce!

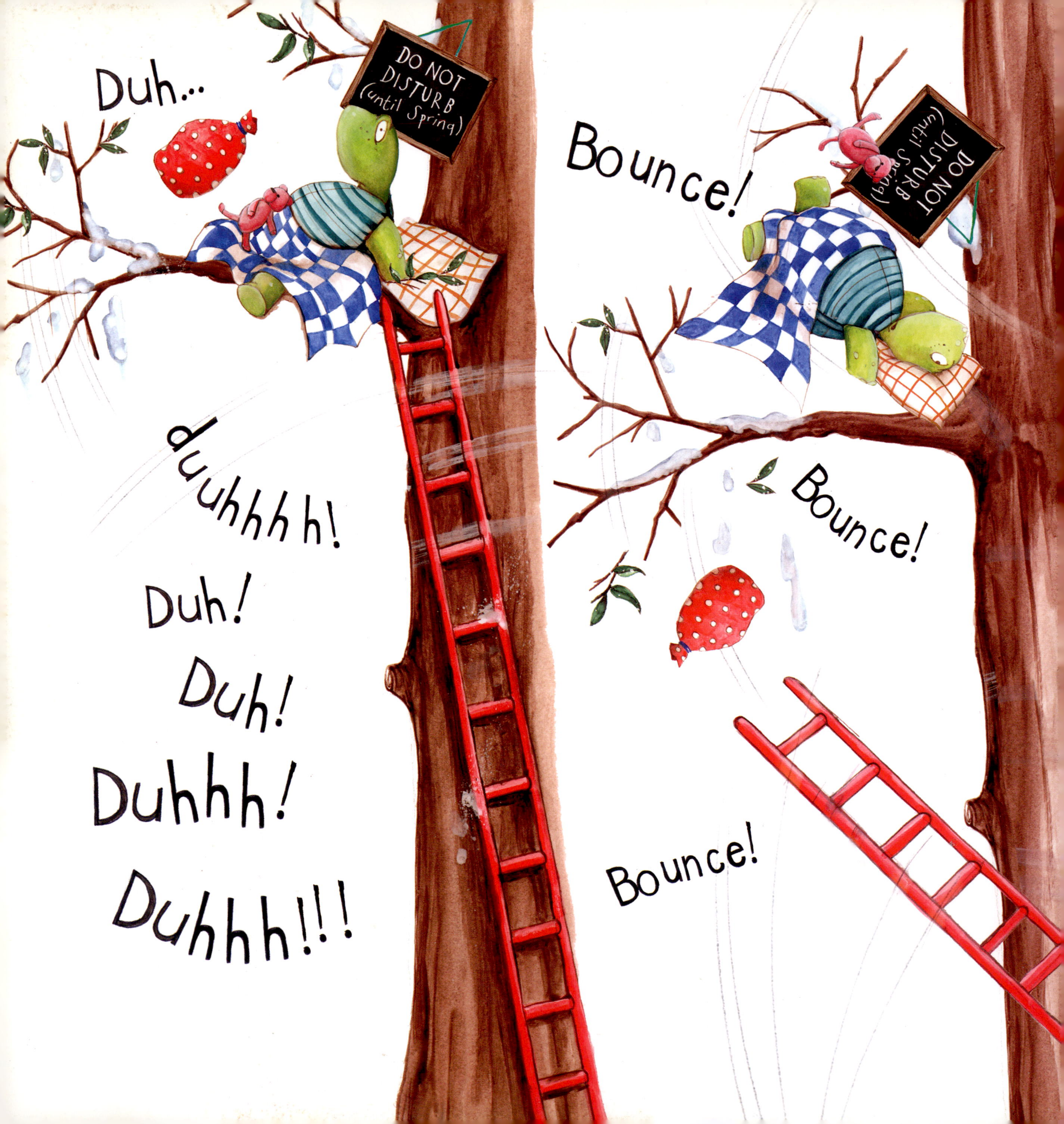

SWISH
SWISH
SWIIISSSSHHH!!!

"Oh, no!" cried Tortoise.

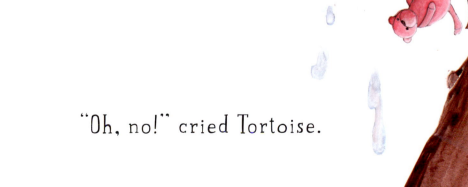

DO NOT
DISTURB
(until Spring)

"I do NOT like winter," Tortoise said.

Tortoise hiked up a big, snowy hill.

Behind a small tree,
Tortoise found a flat
piece of wood. It was the
perfect place for napping!

He snuggled down in his new bed and
was about to close his eyes when ...

Whooosh

As Tortoise whizzed along,
he couldn't help smiling.

Maybe winter isn't so bad?
he thought.

River

ICE
SKATING

And as he flew off his sledge and through the air, he couldn't help giggling.

Maybe winter is more than cold and snow? he thought.

And as he slid across the ice,
he realized he had been wrong.

EEEEEEE E EE!!

That night Tortoise skated, slid,
and spun with his friends late into
the night. He wasn't tired or cold.

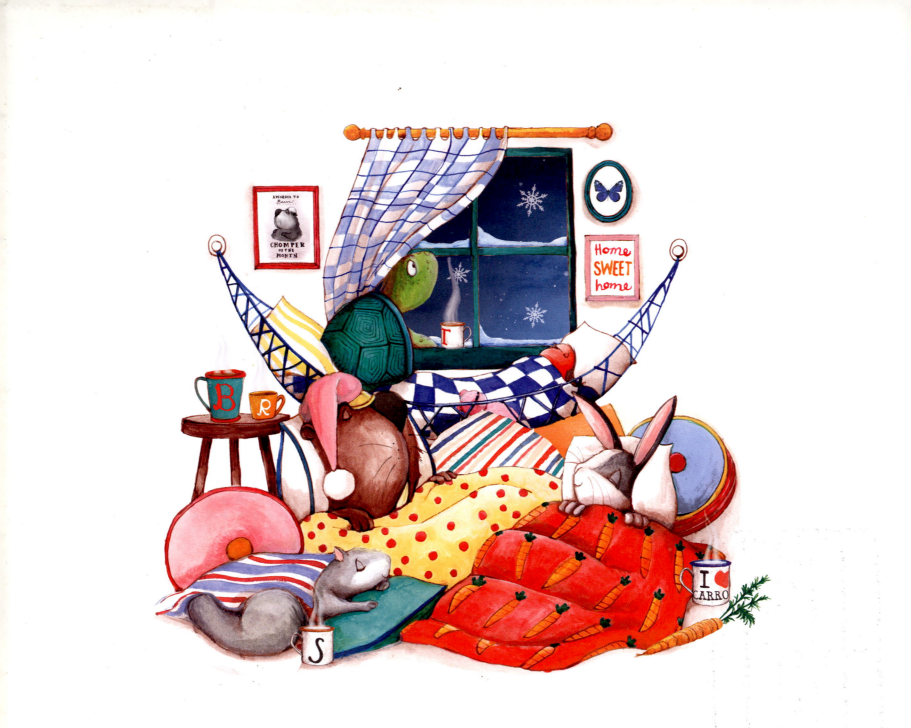

Maybe some tortoises could
like winter after all.